PIRANHAS DON'T EAT BANANAS

For the Gravy Stains.

First published in 2015 by Scholastic Press
An imprint of Scholastic Australia Pty Limited

First published in the UK in 2017 by Scholastic Children's Books
Euston House, 24 Eversholt Street
London NW1 1DB
a division of Scholastic Ltd
www.scholastic.co.uk
London ~ New York ~ Toronto ~ Sydney ~ Auckland
Mexico City ~ New Delhi ~ Hong Kong

ISBN 978 1407 17966 7

10 9 8 7 6 5 4 3 2 1

PIRANHAS DON'T EAT BANANAS

AARON BLABEY

SCHOLASTIC

'Hey there, guys.
Would you like
a banana?'

'What's **wrong** with you, Brian?
You're a piranha.'

'Well,
how about some
silverbeet?'

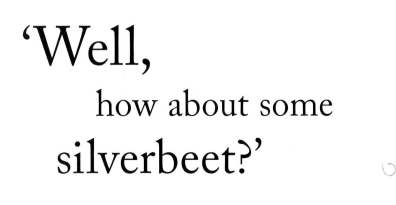

'Are you serious, Brian?
We eat feet.'

'Or would you rather
a bowl of peas?'

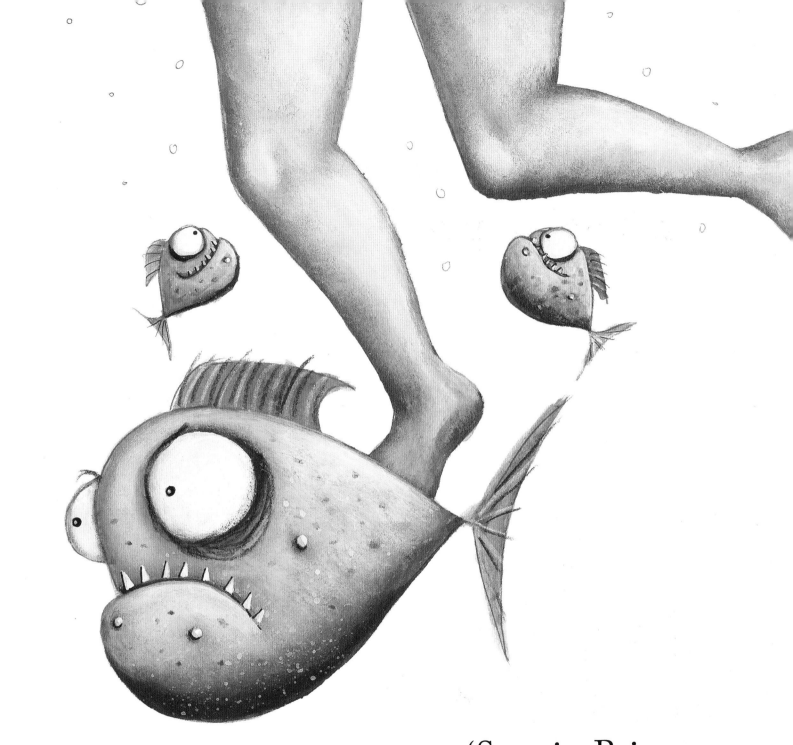

'Stop it, Brian.
We eat knees.'

'Well,
I bet you'd like some
juicy plums?'

'That's *it*, Brian! We eat bums!'

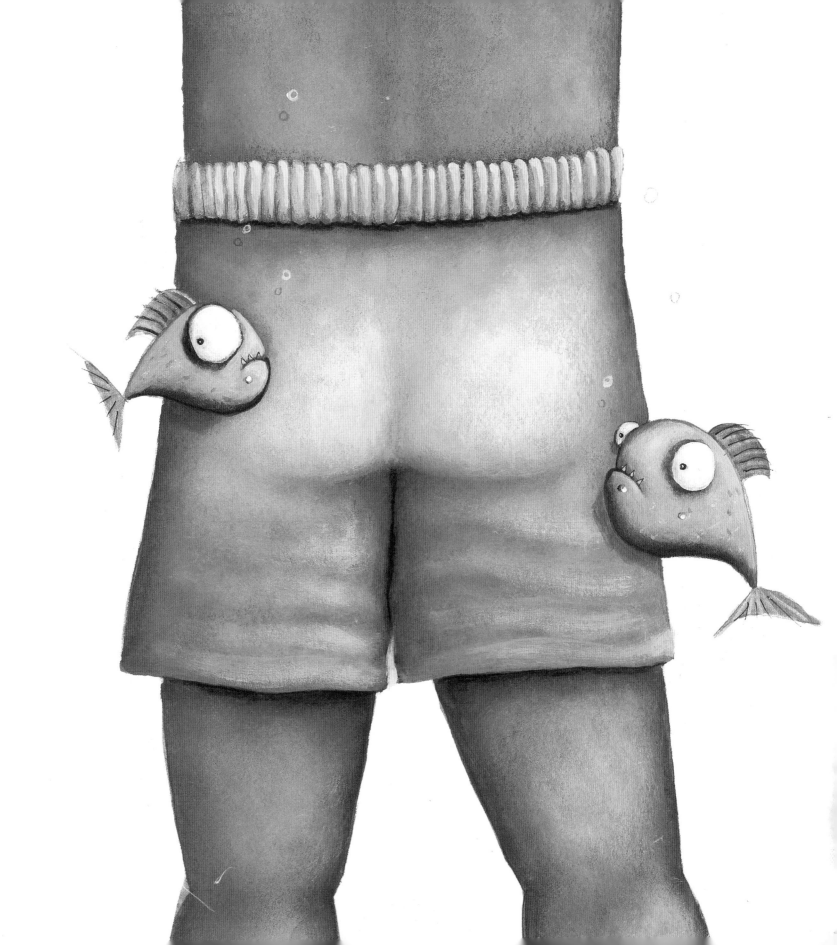

'We don't eat apples!

We don't eat beans!

We don't eat veggies!

We don't eat greens!

We don't eat melons!

We don't eat bananas!

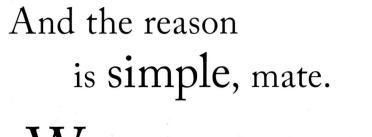

And the reason
is simple, mate.

We are

PIRANHAS!'

'Well, I think
that's silly, guys.
Fruit is the best.'

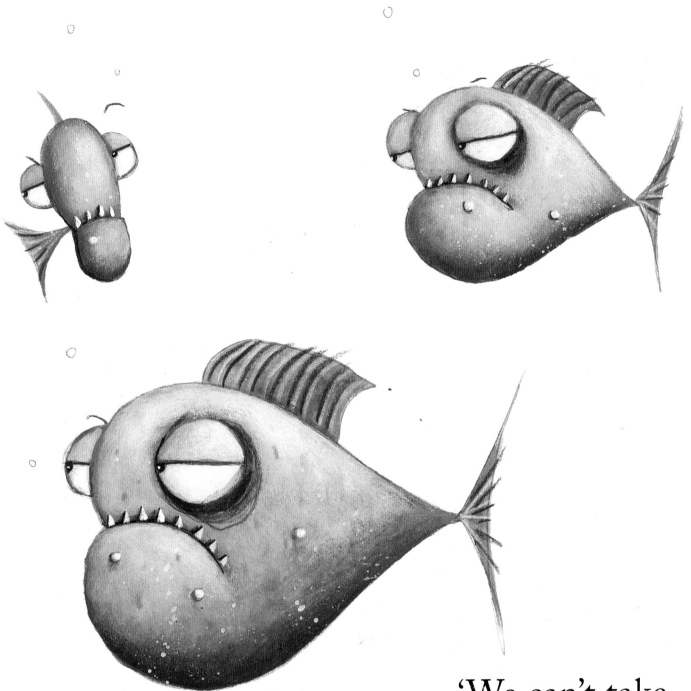

'We can't take
much more of this.
Give it a rest.'

'Okay, I'll stop then.
        You'll hear no more chatter.

But ONLY if you try my
        awesome fruit platter.'

'Give it here, then.'

'So . . .

what do you think, guys?
Is it **yucky** or **yum**?'

'It's very nice,
Brian . . .'

'But we still prefer
bum!'

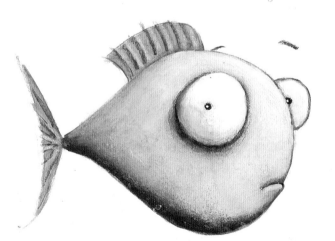